Chart Hits of '01-'02

ISBN 0-634-04481-8

Visit Hal Leonard Online at
www.halleonard.com

ALL OR NOTHING

Words and Music by WAYNE HECTOR
and STEVE MAC

Am7
Fsus2
A♭+
G7sus
G7
some-thing some-where's got to give, as shar-ing this re-la - tion-ship gets old - er, old - er.
though I'm all that you could see. Those times I don't be-lieve it's right, I know it, know it.
F
G
F/A
G/B
C
You know I'd fight for you but how can I fight some-one who is - n't e - ven there?
Don't make me prom-is - es, ba - by; you nev - er did know how to keep them well.
E7/G♯
F/G
I've had the rest of you, now I want the best of you. I don't care if that's not fair.
I've had the rest of you, now I want the best of you; it's time for show and tell.
'Cause I want it
all, or noth - ing at all. There's no - where left to

Am G F G7sus G
fall when you reach the bot - tom; it's now or nev - er. Is it
C G/B
all, or are we just friends? Is this how it
1
Am G F G7sus G
ends, with a sim - ple tel - e-phone call? You leave me here with noth - ing at
C
all.
2
F G7sus G
leave me here with noth - ing. 'Cause

F
G
Am
G/B
C
C/E
you and I could lose it all if you've got no more room, no
F
G
E/G#
F/G
room in sight for me in your life. 'Cause I want it
C
G/B
all, or noth - ing at all. There's no - where left to
Am7
G
F
N.C.
fall; it's now or nev - er. Is it

D
A/C♯
all, or noth - ing at all. There's no - where left to
Bm
A
G
A7sus
A
D
fall when you reach the bot - tom; it's now or nev - er. Is it all, or are we just
A/C♯
Bm
A
G
A7sus
A
friends? Is this how it ends, with a sim - ple tel - e-phone call? You leave me here with noth - ing at
D
A
D/G
A/G
D
all, all.
rit.

FALLIN'

Words and Music by
ALICIA KEYS

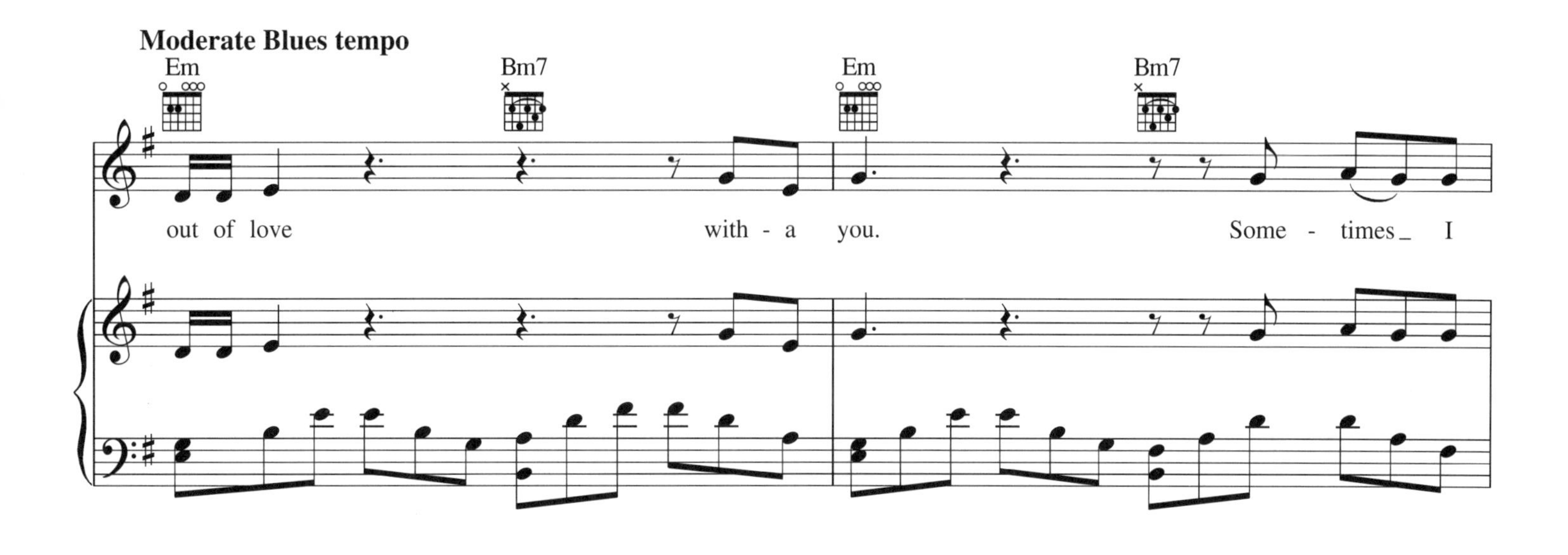

Em Bm7 Em Bm7
good. At times I feel used. Lov - ing you
Em Bm7 Em Bm7
dar - ling makes me so con - fused. I keep on
Em Bm7 Em Bm7
fall - in' in and out of love with - a you. I
Em Bm7 Em Bm7
nev - er loved some - one the way that I love a - you. Oh, oh,

Em
Bm7
I never felt this - a
way.
How do you give me so much
pleas - ure and cause me so much pain?
Yeah, yeah.
Just when I
think
I'm tak - ing more than would a fool,
I start

Em
Bm7
Em
Bm7
fall - in' back in love with you I keep on
Em
Bm7
Em
Bm7
fall - in' in and out of love with - a you. I
Em
Bm7
Em
Em/B
B7#9
nev - er loved some - one the way that I love a - you. Oh ba - by.
Em
Bm7
Em
Bm7
I, I, I, I'm fall - in'.

Em
Bm7
I, I, I, I'm fall - in'.
Fall
fall
fall.
I keep on fall - in' in and out of

Em
Bm7
Em
Bm7
love with - a you. I nev - er loved some - one the way that
Em
Bm7
Em
Bm7
I love a - you. I'm fall - in' in and out of
Em
Bm7
Em
Bm7
love with a - you. I nev - er loved some - one the way that
Em
Bm7
Em
Bm7
I love a - you. I'm fall - in' in and out of

Em
Bm7
Em
Bm7
love with a - you. I nev - er loved some - one the way that
Em
Em/B
N.C.
Em
Bm7
I love a - you. What?
Em
Bm7
Em
Bm7
Em
Bm7
Em

DROPS OF JUPITER
(Tell Me)

Words and Music by PAT MONAHAN,
JIMMY STAFFORD, ROB HOTCHKISS,
CHARLIE COLIN and SCOTT UNDERWOOD

Dm
C/E
with - out a per - ma - nent scar? And did you miss me while you were
ev - ery - thing you want - ed to find and did you miss me while you were
F
To Coda
1
C
G7(no3rd)/D
look - ing for your - self out there?
look - ing for your - self out there?
G5
3 fr
F(add2)
2
C
Now that

G5
3 fr
F(add2)
C
Can you i - mag-ine no love, pride, deep - fried chick-en? Your
G
F(add2)
best friend al - ways stick-ing up for you,
F7sus2
G
C
e - ven when I know you're wrong? Can you i - mag-ine no first dance, freeze - dried, ro - mance,

B♭
five - hour phone con - ver - sa - tion? The best soy lat - te that you
F
G
ev - er had and me? But tell me, did the
G/A
D
C/E
wind sweep you off your feet? Did you fin - ally get the chance to dance
F
C
D.S. al Coda
a - long the light of day and head back toward the Milk - y Way? And

CODA
C
self?
Na na na
G
na na na na na na na na na na
F(add2)
na na na na. And did you fin - ally get the chance to dance a - long the light
C
of day?
Na na na na na na

G
F(add2)
na na na na na na na na na na na.
And did you fall from a
shoot - ing star, fall from a shoot - ing star?
C
G
Na na na na na na na na na
B♭
C/B♭
B♭
F
na na na.
And are you lone - ly look-ing for your - self out there?
rall.

EMOTION

Words and Music by BARRY GIBB
and ROBIN GIBB

G9sus
3 fr
G
C
3
in-stead of me, to - night?
You've got to go find your shin-ing star.
And where are you
3
3
Dm7
Cmaj7
Dm7
now, now that I need you? Tears on my pil - low when-ev - er you go.
Cmaj7
Dm7
Cmaj7
I cry me a riv - er that leads to your o - cean. You'll nev-er see me
G9sus
3 fr
G7
G9sus
3 fr
fall a - part. In the words of a bro - ken heart, it's just e -

Am
Em
mo - tions tak - in' me o - ver.
Caught up in sor -
Am
Em
- row, lost in the song.
But if you don't come
F
Em
Am7
back, come home to me, dar - lin',
(Don't you know there's
C/G
G9sus
3 fr
no - bod - y left in this world to hold me tight,
no - bod - y left in this world to kiss
no
don't you know there's no

1
C
good - night.
kiss good - night?)
(Good-night, good-night.)
Good - night.

G9sus
3fr
2
C
Good - night.
I'm
Good - night.

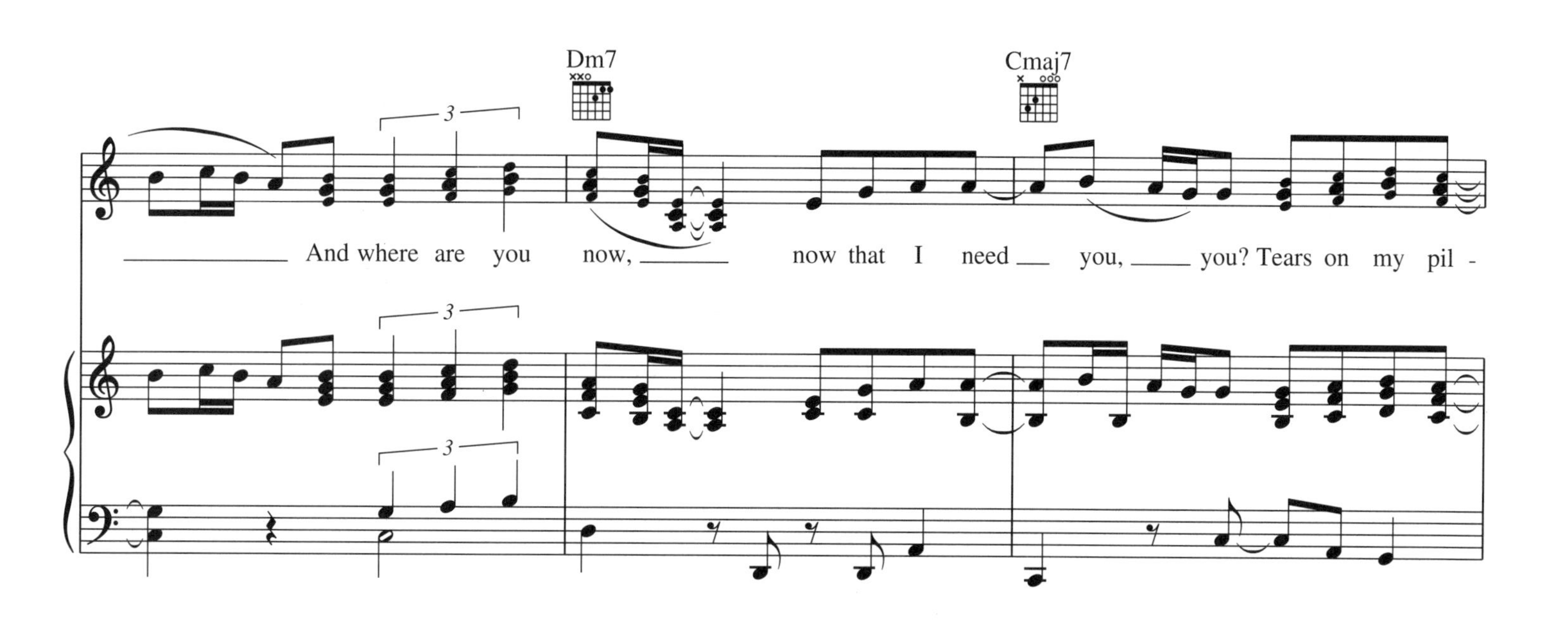
Dm7
Cmaj7
3
And where are you now, now that I need you, you? Tears on my pil -

Dm7
Cmaj7
when - ev - er you, you go.)
- low I cry me a riv -
Dm7
Cmaj7
- er that leads to your o - cean. You'll nev - er see me
G9sus
G
G9sus
3fr
fall a - part. In the words of a bro - ken heart, it's just e -
Am
Em
Am
mo - tions tak - in' me o - ver. I'm caught up in sor - row, lost in the song.
(Lead vocal ad lib.)

Em
F
Em
But if you don't come back, come home to me, dar -
Am7
C/G
G9sus
3 fr
- lin', no - bod - y left in this world to hold me tight,
no - bod - y left in this world to kiss good - night.
C
Good-night, good - night. Good - night.

EVERYWHERE

Words and Music by JOHN SHANKS
and MICHELLE BRANCH

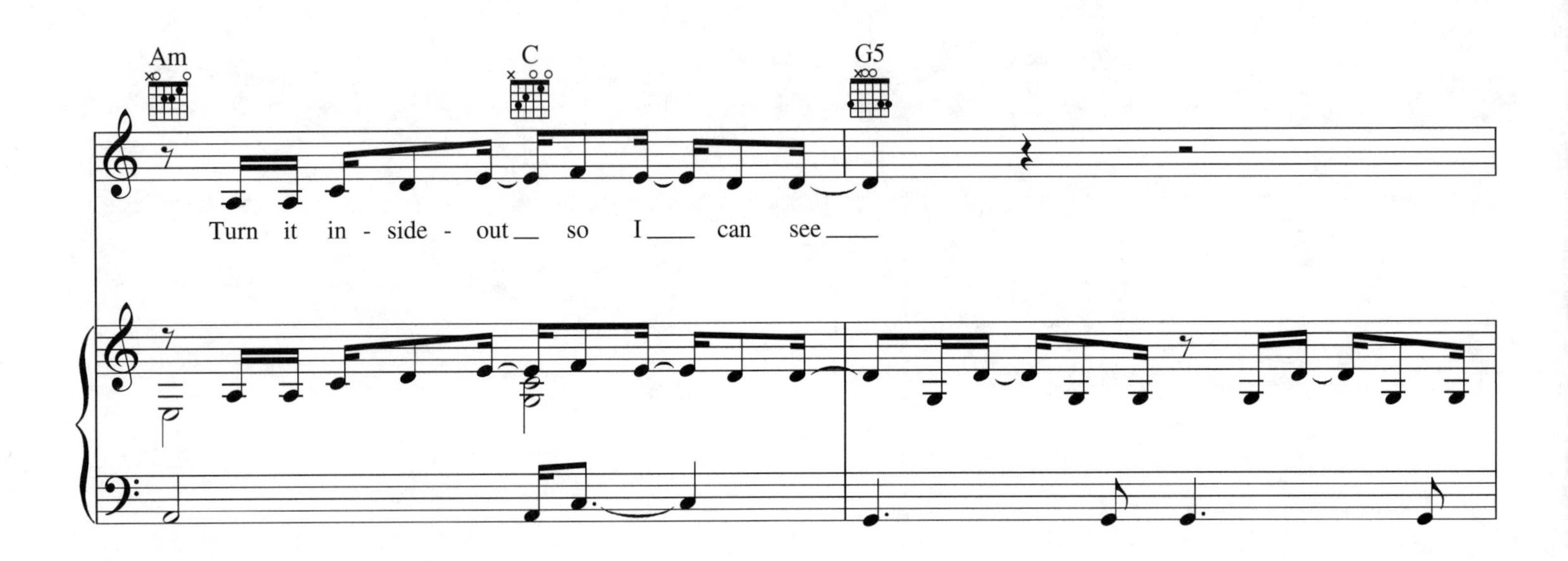

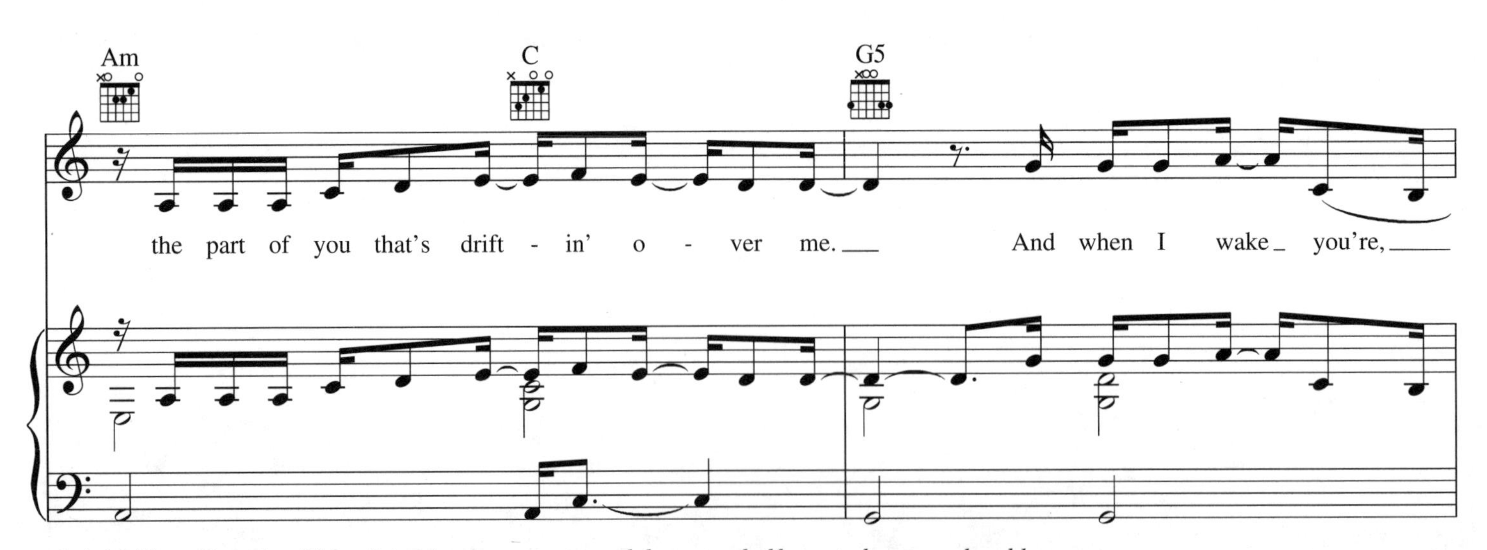

Original key: D♭ major. This edition has been transposed down one half-step to be more playable.

D/F♯
G
you're nev - er there.
And when I sleep you're,
Am
D/F♯
G5
N.C.
you're ev - 'ry - where.
You're ev - 'ry - where.
Am
C
G5
Am
C
G5
Just tell me how I got this far.

Am
C
G5
Just tell me why you're here and who you are. 'Cause ev - 'ry time I look
D/F#
G5
you're al - ways there. And ev - 'ry time I sleep
Am
D/F#
G5
N.C.
you're al - ways there. 'Cause you're
Fsus2
C5
3fr
G5
ev - 'ry - where to me. And when I close my eyes

Fsus2
C5
3fr
G5
it's you I see.
You're ev - 'ry - thing I know.
that makes me be - lieve
I'm not a - lone.
To Coda
N.C.
Am
C
I'm not a - lone.
I re - cog - nize the way you make me feel.

Am
C
G5
It's hard to think that you might not be real.
I sense it now, the wa-
D/F#
G5
-ter's get-ting deep.
I try to wash the pain
E/G#
Am
Am/G
D/F#
D.S. al Coda
N.C.
a-way from me,
a-way from me.
'Cause you're
CODA
Am
D/F#
G
E/G#
Am
D/F#

G E/G♯ Am G/B C G5/D
G5 Fsus2 C5
3fr
When I touch _ your hand, _ it's
G5 Fsus2 C5 G5
then I un - der - stand _ the beau - ty that's _ with - in. _ It's now that we _ be - gin. _ You
Fsus2 C5 G5
al - ways light _ my way. _ I hope there nev - er comes _ a day. _ No

Fsus2
C5
3fr
G5
N.C.
mat - ter where _ I go ___ I al - ways feel __ you so. ___ 'Cause you're
Fsus2
C5
3fr
G
ev - 'ry - where to me. ___
And when I close _ my eyes ___
And when I catch _ my breath _
Fsus2
C5
3fr
G5
___ it's you I see. ______
___ it's you I breathe. _____
You're ev - 'ry - thing _ I know. _
Fsus2
C5
3fr
G5
___ that makes me be - lieve ____ I'm not __ a - lone. _

1
Am
D/F♯
G5
'Cause you're
2
Fsus2
C5
3fr
G5
Oh, you're
Fsus2
C5
3fr
G5
ev - 'ry - one I see.
So tell me,
Fsus2
C5
3fr
G5
do you see me?

FOLLOW ME

Words and Music by MATTHEW SHAFER
and MICHAEL BRADFORD

N.C.
fol - low me ev - 'ry - thing is all right.
I'll be the one to tuck you in at night. And if you want to leave I can
F Bb C F
guar - an - tee you won't find no - bod - y else like me.
Bb F Bb
I'm not wor - ried 'bout the ring you wear 'cause as long as no one knows then no -

C F F Bb
N.C.
bod - y can care. You're feel - ing guil - ty and I'm well a - ware but
F
N.C.
you don't look a - shamed and ba - by I'm not scared. I'm sing - in'
F Bb C F Bb
fol - low me ev - 'ry - thing is all right.
Fol - low me ev - 'ry - thing is all right.
I'll be the one to tuck you
C F Bb C
in at night. And if you want to leave I can guar - an - tee you won't

To Coda
F
B♭
C
F
F/A
Gm
3 fr
find no - bod - y else like me.
Won't give you mon - ey, I can't give you the sky.

F
B♭/F
F
Gm
3 fr
You're bet - ter off if you don't ask why.
I'm not the rea - son that you
G7
C7
D.S. al Coda
go a - stray and we'll be all right if you don't ask me to stay.
CODA
F
B♭
Don't know how you met me. You don't know why you can't
F
B♭
C
F
turn a - round and say good - bye. All you know is when I'm with you I

B♭
F
B♭
C
F
make you free and swim through your veins like a fish in the sea. I'm sing - in'
B♭
C
F
B♭
fol - low me ev - 'ry - thing is all right. I'll be the one to tuck you
C
F
B♭
in at night. And if you want to leave I can
C
F
B♭
C
F
guar - an - tee you won't find no - bod - y else like me. I'm sing - in'

B♭
C
fol - low me ev - 'ry - thing is all right.
F
B♭
C
I'll be the one to tuck you in at night. And if you
F
B♭
C
want to leave I can guar - an - tee you won't
F
B♭
C
F
find no - bod - y else like me.

GET THE PARTY STARTED

Words and Music by
LINDA PERRY

* Vocal written one octave higher than sung.

N.C.
Bm
Get this par - ty start - ed on a Sat - ur - day night. Ev - 'ry - bod - y's
vol - ume, break - in' down to the beat. Cruis - in' through the
nec - tion as I en - ter the room. Ev - 'ry - bod - y's
wait - in' for me to ar - rive. Send - in' out the mes - sage to all of my friends.
west side we'll be check - in' the scene. Bou - le - vard is freak - in' as I'm com - in' up fast.
chill - in' as I set up the groove. Pump - in' up the vol - ume with this brand new beat.
We'll be look - in' flash - y in my Mer - ced - es Benz. I get lots of
I'll be burn - in' rub - ber, you'll be kiss - in' my ass. Pull up to the
Ev - 'ry - bod - y's danc - in' and they're danc - in' for me. I'm your op - er -
style, got my gold dia - mond rings. I can go for miles if you know what I mean.
bump - er, get out of the car. Li - cense plate says "Stunn - er Num - ber One Sup - er - star."
a - tor, you can call an - y - time. I'll be your con - nec - tion to the par - ty line.

To Coda
I'm
com - in' up so you
bet - ter get this par - ty start - ed.
I'm com - in' up
I'm com - in'.
I'm
com - in' up so you bet - ter get this par - ty start - ed.
Pump - in' up the
Get this par - ty
start - ed.

Bm9
Bm
Bm9
Bm
N.C.
D.S. al Coda
Mak - in' my con-
CODA
I'm com - in' up so you bet - ter get this par - ty start - ed
Play 3 times
I'm com - in' up,
uh huh.
I'm com - in'.
you bet - ter.
I'm com - in' up so you
bet - ter get this par - ty start - ed. Get this par - ty start - ed.

Get this par - ty start - ed right now. Get this par - ty
start - ed. Get this par - ty start - ed.
Get this par - ty start - ed right now.
N.C.

HERO

Words and Music by ENRIQUE IGLESIAS,
PAUL BARRY and MARK TAYLOR

Csus2
Dsus
run and nev - er look back? Would you
G5
3fr
Em7
cry if you saw me cry - ing? Would you
Csus2
Dsus
G5
3fr
save my soul to - night? Would you
G5
3fr
Em7
trem - ble if I touched your lips? Would you
swear that you'll al - ways be mine? Would you

Csus2
Dsus
D
laugh? Oh, please tell me this. Now would you die
lie? Would you run and hide? Am I in too deep?
G5
Em7
for the one you love? Hold me
Have I lost my mind? I don't
Csus2
Dsus
G5
in your arms to - night.
care, you're here to - night.
D
Csus2
D/F#
I can be your he - ro ba - by.

G
Dsus
Csus2
D/F♯
I can kiss a - way the pain.
To Coda
G
D
Csus2
D/F♯
I will stand by you for - ev - er.
G
D
C(add2)
You can take my breath a - way.
1
Would you
2
3

Em9
Csus2
Dsus
G5
3fr
Em7
Oh, I just want to hold you.
Csus2
Dsus
I just want to hold you, oh yeah. Am I in too deep?

G(add2)
Em7
Have I lost my mind? Well, I don't
Csus2
Dsus
G5
3fr
D.S. al Coda
care you're here to - night.
CODA
G
D
C(add2)
C/E
D
You can take my breath a - way.
D
Csus2
C/E
D/F♯
I can be your he - ro ba - by.

G
Dsus
Csus2
C/E
D/F♯
I can kiss a - way the pain. and I will
G
D
Csus2
C/E
D/F♯
stand by you for - ev - er.
G
D
Csus2
You can take my breath a - way.
G
D
Csus2
I can be your he - ro.

IF YOU'RE GONE

Written by ROB THOMAS

E
A
Dsus2
I think you're wrong.
I think you're al - read - y leav -
F♯m
Esus
Dsus2
- ing,
feels like your hand is on the door.
A
A/C♯
D
A/C♯
Bm7
2 fr
I thought this place was an em - pire,
now I'm re - laxed,
I can't be sure.
E
Bm
And I think you're so mean,
I think we should try.

E
A
D
A/C♯
Bm
I think I could need this in my life and I think I'm scared,
I think too much.
G
I know it's wrong, it's a prob-
lem I'm deal-ing. If you're gone,
may-be it's time to come home.
There's an aw-ful lot of breath-ing room,

E
A
but I can hard - ly move.
If you're gone,
D
ba - by, you need to come home,
come
A/C♯
Bm
E
To Coda
home. There's a lit - tle bit of some-thing me
in ev - 'ry-thing in
Asus2
Dsus2
F♯m
E
D(add2)
you.

A
Dsus2
F#m
Esus
Dsus2
I bet you're hard to get o - ver,
I bet the room just won't
A
A/C#
Dsus2
A/C#
Bm
shine.
I bet my hands I can stay here and I bet you need
E
more than you mind.
And I think you're so mean,
Bm
E
A
D
I think we should try.
I think I could need this in my life.

A/C#
Bm
E
I think I'm just scared that I know too much. I
G
D.S. al Coda
can't re - late and that's a prob - lem I'm feel - ing. If you're gone,
CODA
Bm
E7
A
D
you.
A/C#
Bm
E7

A
I think you're so mean,
Bm
I think we should try.
E
I think I could need
A
this in my life
D
A/C♯
and I think I'm
Bm
scared.
Do I talk too much?
E
I know it's
G
wrong. It's a prob -

A
lem I'm deal-ing. If you're gone, then may-be it's time to come home.
D
A/C♯
Bm
Well, there's an aw - ful lot of breath - ing room,
E
A
but I can hard - ly move.
And, if you're gone,
yeah, ba - by, you need to come home,

D
A/C#
ooh, come home. There's a lit - tle
Bm
E
bit of some - thing me in ev - 'ry - thing in
Bm
E
Bm
you. Some - thing in
E
Bm
E
A
me, ev - 'ry - thing in, some - thing in me in you.
rit.

HIT 'EM UP STYLE (OOPS!)

Words and Music by
DALLAS AUSTIN

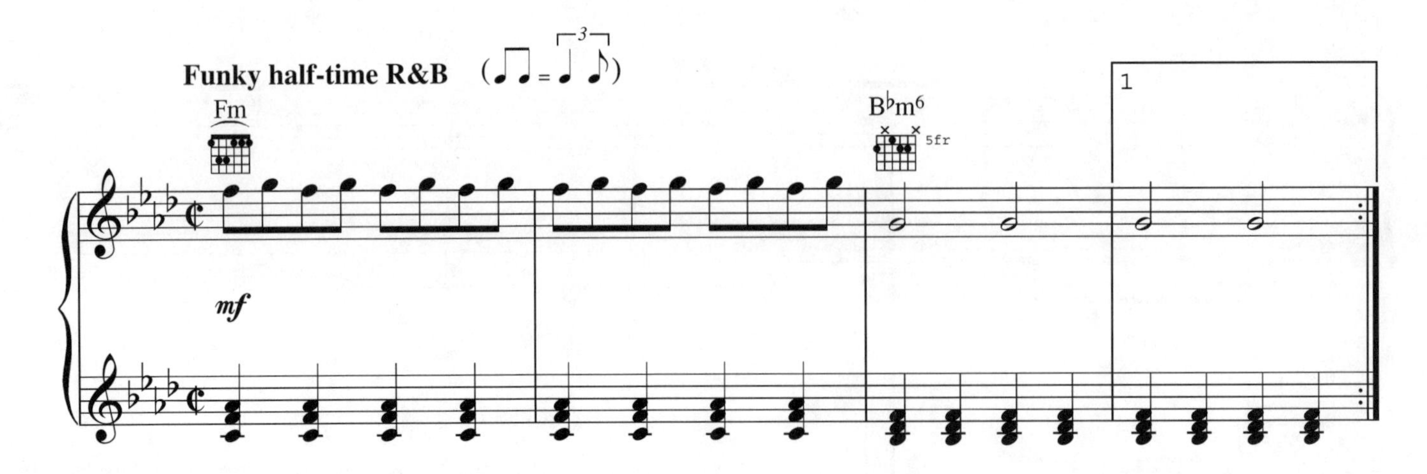

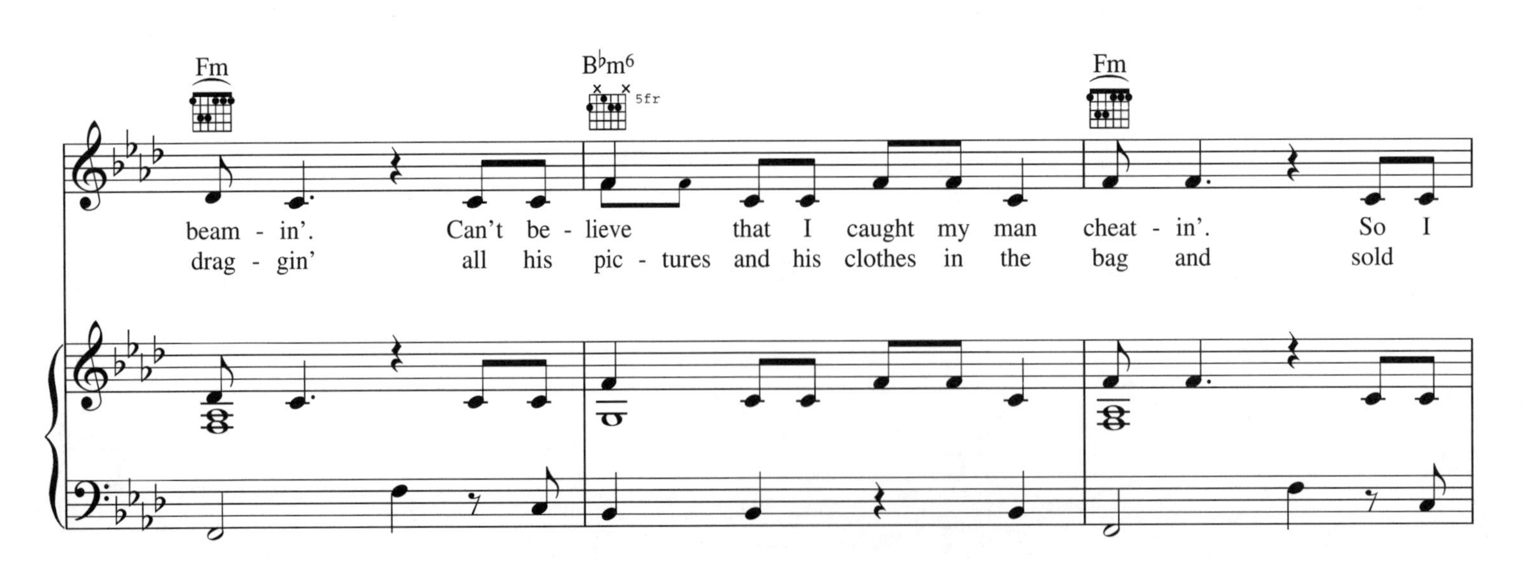

B♭m6 5fr
Fm
B♭m6 5fr
C5 3fr
found an - oth - er way to make him pay for it all. So I
ev - 'ry - thing else 'til there was just noth - in' left. And I
Fm
B♭m6 5fr
Fm
went to Nie - man - Mar - cus on a shop - ping spree - ah, and on the
paid all the bills a - bout a month too late. It's a
B♭m6 5fr
Fm
B♭m6 5fr
way I grabbed Sol - ey and Mi - a. And as the cash box rang I
shame we have to play these games. The love we had just
Fm
B♭m6/F
Fm
Oops.
thought ev - 'ry - thing a - way.
fades a - way, a - way.
There goes the

B♭m6
5fr
Fm
B♭m6
5fr
Oops.
dreams we used to say. There goes the time we spent a -
Fm
B♭m6
5fr
Fm
Oops.
way. There goes the love I had, but you cheat - ed on me and
B♭m6
C5
3fr
Fm
B♭m6
5fr
Oops.
that's for that now. There goes the house we made a
Fm
B♭m6
5fr
Fm
Oops.
Oops.
home. There goes you'll nev - er leave me a - lone. For all the

B♭m6
5fr
Fm
lies you told, this is what you owe. Hey
la - dies, when your man wan - na get buck - wild, just
go back and hit 'em up style. Put your hands on his cash and
spend it to the last dime for all the hard times. Oh, when you

B♭m6
Fm
5fr
go then ev - 'ry - thing goes, from the crib to the ride and the
clothes. So you bet - ter let him know that if he mess up, you got -
To Coda
3
1
B♭m6/F
C5/F
- ta hit 'em up.
While he was
2
D.S. al Coda
- ta hit 'em up. Hey

CODA
B♭m6/F
C5/F
Fm
- ta hit 'em up.
All of the dreams you sold
Fm/E♭
left me out in the cold.
What hap - pened to the
Fm/C
Cm7
Fm/C
days when we used to trust each oth - er?
And all of the things I sold

Fm/E♭
Fm
will take you un - til you get old to get 'em back
Fm/C
C
with - out me, 'cause it might be just bet - ter than mon - ey you'll see. Hey
Fm
B♭m6
5fr
Fm
la - dies, when your man wan - na get buck - wild, just
B♭m6
5fr
Fm
B♭m6
5fr
go back and hit 'em up style. Put your hands on his cash and

Fm
B♭m6
5fr
Fm
spend it to the last dime for ___ all the hard times. Oh, when you
B♭m6
5fr
Fm
B♭m6
5fr
go then ev - 'ry - thing goes, from the crib to the ride and the
Fm
B♭m6
5fr
Fm
3
clothes. So you bet - ter let him know that if he mess up, you got -
Repeat and Fade
B♭m6
5fr
C5
3fr
- ta hit 'em up. Hey
Optional Ending
B♭m6
5fr
C5
3fr
Fm
- ta hit 'em up. ___

I HOPE YOU DANCE

Words and Music by TIA SILLERS
and MARK D. SANDERS

Gm7
You get your fill to eat, but al - ways keep that
Nev - er set - tle for the path of least re -
hun - ger.
sis - tence.
Eb
May you nev - er take one
Liv - in' might mean tak - in'
sin - gle breath for grant - ed.
chanc - es if they're worth tak - in'.
God for - bid
Lov - in' might
F
love ev - er leave you emp - ty hand - ed.
be a mis - take, but it's worth mak - in'.

E♭
F
I hope you still feel small when you stand be - side the
Don't let some hell - bent heart leave you
B♭
E♭
F
o - cean. When - ev - er one door clos - es, I
bit - ter. When you come close to sell - in' out,
B♭
hope one more o - pens. Prom - ise me
re - con - sid - er. Give the heav -
Cm7
B♭/D
that you'll give faith a fight - ing
- ens a - bove more than just a pass - ing

E♭
3 fr
chance.
glance.
And when you get the choice to
To Coda
Fsus
F
sit it out or dance,
I hope you dance.
1
Gm
E♭
B♭
F/A
I hope you dance.
Gm
E♭

Fsus
F
I hope you
2
Gm
Eb
Time is a
wheel in con - stant mo - tion, al - ways roll -
Bb
F/A
I hope you
Gm
Eb
- ing us a - long.
dance.
Fsus
F
Gm
Eb
Tell me, who wants to
I hope you dance.

B♭
F/A
look back on their youth and won - der where
I hope you
Gm
E♭
Fsus
F
those years have gone?
dance.
D.S. al Coda
I hope you still
CODA
Fsus
N.C.
dance.
Gm
E♭
B♭
F/A
Dance,

Gm
E♭
I hope you dance.
Fsus
F
Gm
E♭
Time is a
I hope you dance.
B♭
F/A
wheel in con - stant mo - tion, al - ways roll -
I hope you
Gm
E♭
- ing us a - long.
dance.

Fsus
F
Gm
Eb
Tell me, who wants to
I hope you dance.
Bb
F/A
look back on their youth and won - der where
I hope you
Gm
Eb
Repeat and Fade
Fsus
F
those years have gone?
dance.
Optional Ending
Fsus
F
Bb
I hope you dance.
rit.

I'M REAL

Words and Music by JENNIFER LOPEZ,
CORY ROONEY, TROY OLIVER
and MARTIN DENNY

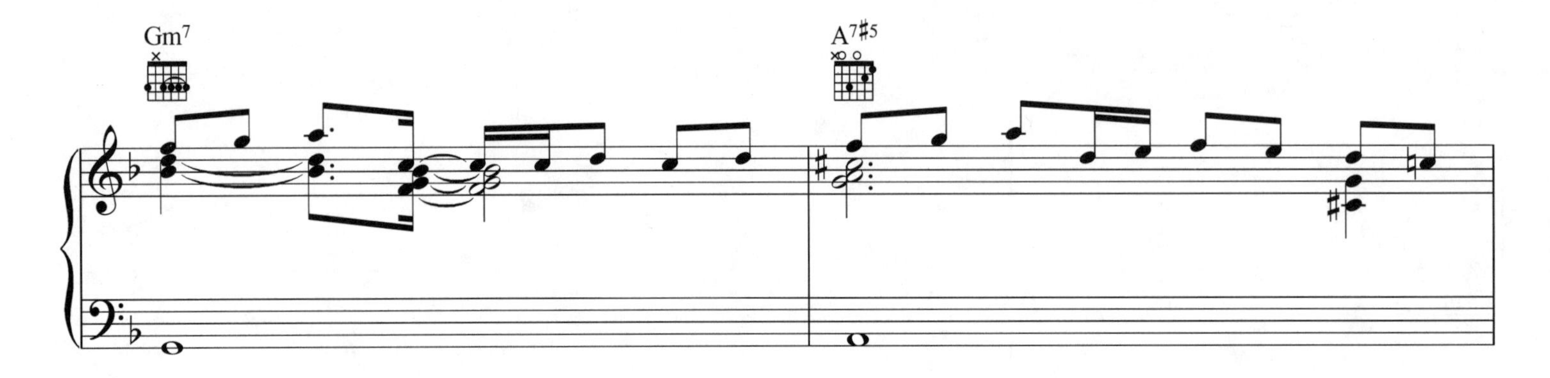

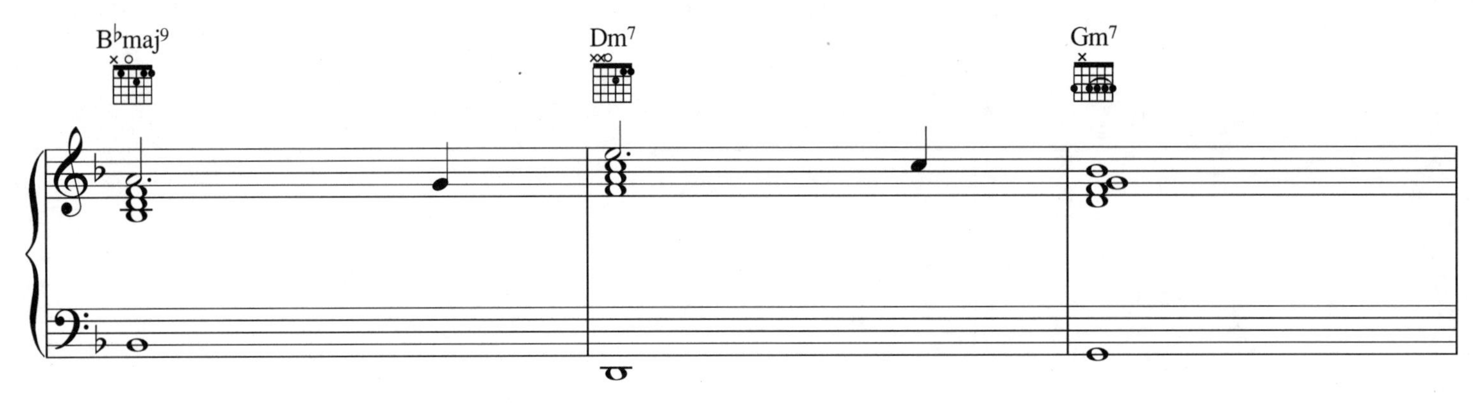

Uh, uh!
Let's go!
Called you on the phone, said I'm com - in' through. Hope you're all a -
You like the way I dress, the way I wear my hair. Show me off to all your
lone 'cause I got plans for you. We could stay at home or dance and hang all
friends and ba - by I don't care. Just as long as you tell them who I
night. As long as I'm with you, does - n't mat - ter what we do.
am Tell them I'm the one who made you give a damn!
Don't ask me where

I've been or what I'm gon - na do. Just know that I'm here with you.
Don't try to un - der - stand. Ba - by, there's no mys - ter - y 'cause you
B♭
Dm
know how I am. I'm real. What you get is what you see. What you try'n to do to
Gm7
A7
B♭
me? You wan - na say you're mine, be with me all the time. You're fall - in' so in

Dm
Gm7
1
A7♯5
love. Say you just can't get e - nough. You're tell - in' all your friends, "She's a bad, bad
N.C.
bitch!" Ooh, come on, come on!
2
A7♯5
B♭
Huh, in the pock - et yeah! friends, "She's a bad, bad bitch!"
I'm real. What you get is what you
Dm
Gm7
A7♯5
see. What you try'n to do to me? You wan - na say you're mine, be with me all the

B♭
Dm
Gm7
To Coda
time. You're fall - in' so in love. Say you just can't get e - nough. You're tell - in' all your
A7♯5
N.C.
friends, "She's a bad, bad bitch!"

I'm
B♭
Dm
Gm7
real. What you get is what you see. What you try'n to do to me? You wan - na say you're
A7♯5
B♭
Dm
mine, be with me all the time. You're fall - in' so in love. Say you just can't get e -
Gm7
A7♯5
B♭
nough. You're tell - in' all your friends, "She's a bad, bad bitch!"
I'm real. What you get is what you

Dm
Gm7
A7♯5
see. What you try'n to do to me? You wan - na say you're mine, be with me all the
B♭
Dm
Gm7
time. You're fall - in' so in love. Say you just can't get e - nough. You're tell - in' all your
A7♯5
N.C.
D.S. al Coda
(take 2nd ending)
friends, "She's a bad bad bitch!" Don't ask me where
CODA
A7♯5
B♭
Dm
friends, "She's a bad, bad bitch!"
I'm real. What you get is what you see. What you try'n to do to

Gm7
A7#5
B♭
me? You wan - na say you're mine, be with me all the time. You're fall - in' so in
Dm
Gm7
A7
love. Say you just can't get e - nough. You're tell - in' all your friends, "She's a bad, bad
B♭
Dm
bitch!" (1st time only)
Gm7
A7#5
Repeat and Fade
Optional Ending
Dm

LADY MARMALADE

from the Motion Picture MOULIN ROUGE

Words and Music by BOB CREWE
and KENNY NOLAN

Moderate Funk

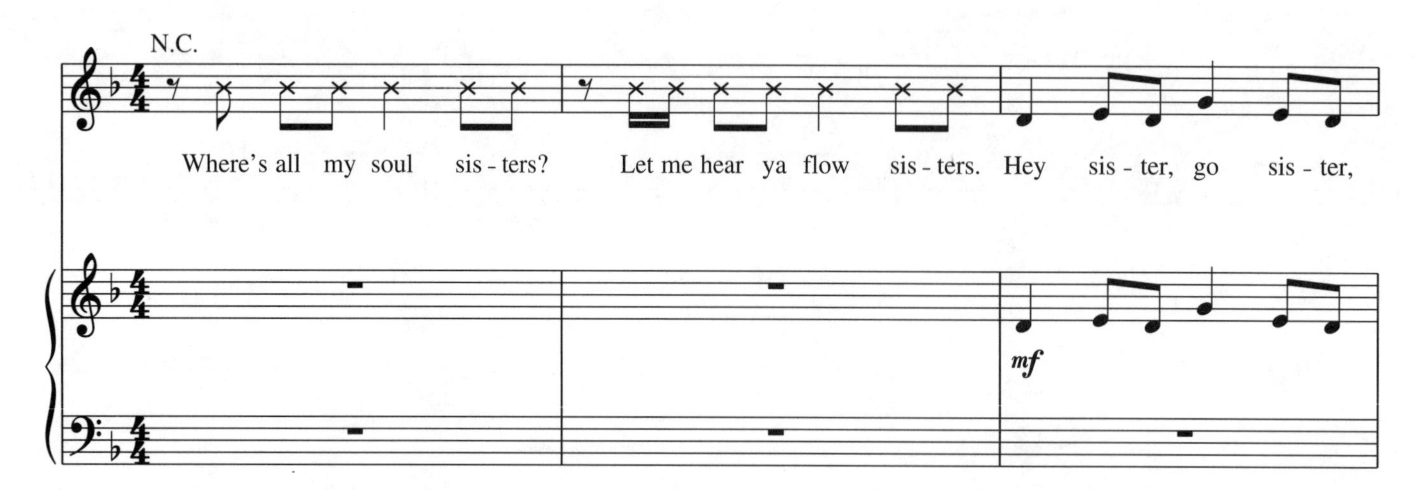

Cm7
3fr
She said, "Hel - lo, hey Joe, you wan - na
D7♯9
4fr
give it a go?" Oh, uh!
Gm7
C7
Git - chie, git - chie, ya - ya, da
da.
Gm7
C7
Git - chie, git - chie, ya - ya here.
Gm7
C7
Mo - cha cho - co - la - ta ya ya.
C5
3fr
N.C.
Cre - ole La - dy Mar - ma - lade,

Gm7
C7
ooh.
Vou - lez vous cou - cher av - ec moi
To Coda
ce - soir? Ahh!
Vou - lez vous cou - cher av - ec moi? Yeah, yeah, yeah, yeah! He
N.C.
sat in her bou - doir while she fresh - ened up.
Boy drank all that mag -
Cm7
D7#9
D.S. al Coda
no - lia wine. On her black sat - in sheets, where he start - ed to freak yeah.

CODA
N.C.
Gm
3 fr
Yeah, yeah, oh, we come through with the mon-ey in the gar - ter belts. Let 'em
N.C.
Gm
3 fr
know we 'bout that cake, straight out the gate. We in-de-pen-dent wom-en, some mis-take us for whores. I'm say-in',
N.C.
Gm
3 fr
why spend mine when I can spend yours? Dis - a - gree? Well that's you and I'm sor - ry. I'm - a
(When I can spend yours)
N.C.
Gm
3 fr
keep play-in' these cats out like A - tar - i. Wear high heel shoes, get-tin' love from the dudes. Four

Gm
3 fr
N.C.
bad - ass chicks from the Mou - lin Rouge. Hey sis - ters, soul sis - ters,
bet - ter get that dough sis - ters. We drink wine with dia - monds in the glass. By the
case, the mean - ing of ex - pen - sive taste. We wan - na git - chie, git - chie ya - ya. C'- mon
C5
mo - cha cho - co - la - ta, what? Cre - ole La - dy Mar - ma - lade.

Gm
F/G
3 fr
One more time, c' - mon now. Mar - ma - lade, La - dy
G
Mar - ma - lade.
Gm
F/G
Mar - ma - lade, ooh,
D
yeah! Hey, hey, hey!
Gm7
C7
Touch of her skin feel - in' silk - y smooth, hey!
Gm7
C9
Col - or of ca - fé au lait,

Cm7
3 fr
D7#9
4 fr
D7
alright. Made the sav - age beast in-side roar un-til he cried more,
Gm7
C7
more, more! Now he's back home do-in' nine
(More) (More)
Gm7
C7
to five, liv - in' a gray flan - nel life. But when he
Cm7
3 fr
D7#9
4 fr
D7
turns off to sleep, mem - o - ries creep. More, more more!
(More) (More)

Gm7
C7
Git-chie, git-chie ya-ya da da.
Gm7
C7
Gm7
C7
Git-chie, git-chie ya-ya here.
Mo-cha cho-co-la-ta ya
ya.
Cm
3fr
N.C.
Cre-ole La-dy Mar - ma-lade.
Gm7
C7
Vou-lez vous cou-cher av-ec moi ce-soir? Ce-soir!

Gm7
C7
Vou-lez vous cou-cher av-ec moi? All my sis-ters, yeah! Vou-lez vous cou-cher av-ec moi
ce-soir? Ce-soir! Vou-lez vous cou-cher av-ec moi? C'-mon uh!
N.C.
Chris-tin-a. Hey
ooh! Pink. La-dy Mar-ma-lade! Lil' Kim. Hey,

Gm7
C7
Gm7
C7
hey oh, oh, oh, oh, oh, oh, oh! My - a. Oh, oh, oh!
Gm7
C7
Rott-weil-er ba-by. La - dy! Mou-lin Rouge. Ooh!
Gm7
C7
Cm7
3fr
Gm7
Da, da, da, da! Mis-de-mean-or here! Cre-ole La-dy Mar - ma - lade,
G
ooh, yes ah!

NOBODY WANTS TO BE LONELY

Words and Music by DESMOND CHILD,
VICTORIA SHAW and GARY BURR

Original key: B♭ minor. This edition has been transposed down one half-step to be more playable.

N.C.
There you are in a dark - ened room. And you're all a - lone look-ing
Am
G
out the win - dow. Your heart is cold and lost the will to love
Dm9
F
E
F
like a bro - ken ar - row. Here I stand in the
C
F
G
shad - ows. Come to me, come to me. Both: Can't you see that,

Am
G
Dm9
No - bod - y wants to be lone - ly.
No - bod - y wants
F
Am
G
to cry.
My bod - y's long - ing to hold you
Dm9
F
C5
3 fr
so bad it hurts in - side.
Time is pre-cious and it's
G/B
Dm
F
slip-ping a - way and I've been wait-ing for you all of my life.

Am
G
To Coda
No - bod - y wants to be lone - ly. Male: So
Dm9
C/E
F
Am
why,
why don't you let me love you? (Why?)
G
Dm7
F
E
(Why?)
(Why?)
Female: Can you
Am
G
hear my voice?
Do you hear my song?
It's a

Fmaj7
G
ser - e - nade so your heart can find me, ooh.
Am
G
And sud - den - ly you're fly - ing down the stairs
F
E
in - to my arms ba - by, ooh.
F
C
Male: Be - fore I start go - ing cra - zy

D.S. al Coda
F
G
run to me, Female: run to me Both: 'cause I'm dy - ing.
CODA
Dm9
C/E
F
why, Female: why, why don't you let me love
Fmaj7
C/E
you? Male: I wan-na feel you near me just like the
Am
air you're breath - ing. Female: I need you

Gsus
3 fr
here in my life. Both: Don't walk a - way Female: Don't walk a - way. Male: Don't
G
Fmaj7
walk a - way, walk a - way no, no. Female: No - bod - y wants to be lone - ly.
Dm9
F
Both: No - bod - y wants to cry.
Am
G
No - bod - y wants to be lone - ly.

Dm9
F
No - bod - y wants to cry.
Am
G
My bod - y's long - ing to hold you
Dm9
F
so bad it hurts in - side.
C5
3 fr
G/B
Time is pre - cious and it's slip - ping a - way and I've been

Dm
F
wait - ing for you all of my life.
Am
G
No - bod - y wants to be lone - ly. Male: So
Dm9
C/E
F
why, why, why don't you let me love
Repeat and Fade
Optional Ending
Am
Am
you? Both: No - bod - y wants you?

THERE YOU'LL BE

from Touchtone Pictures'/Jerry Bruckheimer Films' PEARL HARBOR

Words and Music by
DIANE WARREN

E♭/G
D♭
D♭sus2
A♭/C
G♭/B♭
A♭/C
D♭
E♭
look and see your face.
owe so much to you.
You were right there for me.
Fm
Cm/E♭
D♭maj7
D♭6
Cm7
A♭/C
In my dreams I'll al - ways see you soar a - bove the sky.
Fm
Cm/E♭
D♭maj7
E♭
In my heart there'll al - ways be a place for you, for all my life.
1
A♭
E♭/G
Fm
Cm/E♭
I'll keep a part of you with me, and ev -

Db Ab/C Bbm7 Absus Ab Bbm Ab/C
3 fr
4 fr
- 'ry - where I am, there you'll be, and ev -
Db Ab/C Bbm7 Ab Gb(add2) Db/F
- 'ry-where I am there you'll be. Well, you
2
Ab Eb/G Fm Eb6
I'll keep a part of you with me, and ev -
Db Ab/C Bbm7 Eb Ab
- 'ry - where I am, there you'll be. 'Cause I al-ways saw in you my light,

D♭/F
E♭/G
A♭
E♭
A♭
Fm7
D♭maj7
my strength,
and I wan-na thank you now for all the ways
D♭(add2)
A♭/C
B♭m7
A♭/C
D♭(add2)
you were right there for me.
You were right there for me, for
E♭
Fm
Cm/E♭
al - ways.
In my dreams I'll al - ways see you
D♭maj7
D♭6
Cm7
A♭/C
B♭m11
E♭6
soar a - bove the sky.
In my heart there'll al - ways be a place

D♭maj7
A♭
E♭/G
for you for all my life. I'll keep a part
Fm
Cm/E♭
D♭
A♭/C
B♭m7
of you with me, and ev - 'ry - where I am, there you'll be,
A♭sus
A♭
B♭m7
A♭/C
D♭
A♭/C
B♭m7
A♭
and ev - 'ry - where I am, there you'll be.
Freely
G♭maj9♯11
A♭(add2)
There you'll be.

ONLY TIME

Words and Music by ENYA,
NICKY RYAN and ROMA RYAN

Cm
3fr
A♭
4fr
De da da day.
De da da day.
B♭
E♭
B♭/D
Cm
3fr
De da day.
De da da da da de.
A♭
4fr
B♭
Oh da day.
De da da day da day.
E♭
Cm
3fr
A♭
4fr
Who can say when the roads meet that love might be on your
Who can say if your love grows as your heart chose? On - ly

E♭
Cm
3fr
heart? And who can say when the day sleeps if the
time. And who can say where the road goes, where the
A♭
4fr
E♭
To Coda
A♭
4fr
night keeps all your heart? Night keeps all your
day flows? On - ly time.
E♭
F♯
C♯
B
heart.
De da da
F♯
C♯
B
F♯
day. Da da da day.

C♯
B
F♯
De da da day.
C♯
B
B♭
De da da da
E♭
D.S. al Coda
oh.
CODA
A♭
4fr
Who knows? On - ly
E♭
A♭
4fr
E♭
time.
Who knows? On - ly time.

SOMEONE TO CALL MY LOVER

Words and Music by JAMES HARRIS III,
TERRY LEWIS, JANET JACKSON
and DEWEY BUNNELL

- contains elements of "Ventura Highway" by Dewey Bunnell

Dmaj7
to be mine. Friends say I'm cra - zy 'cause eas - i - ly I fall in love. "You
but I'm blind. I love hard with ev - 'ry - thing, giv - ing my all, more than they. I'll
G
Dmaj7
got - ta do it dif - f'rent ly this time."
take my friends' ad - vice this time. I'll do it dif - f'rent - ly.
May - be we'll meet at a bar.
Gmaj7
He'll drive a funk - y car. May - be we'll meet at a club and fall so deep - ly in love.
Dmaj7
Gmaj7
He'll tell me I'm the one and we'll have so much fun. I'll be the girl of his dreams,

Dmaj7
may - be. Al - right, may - be gon - na find him to - day. I got - ta
Gmaj7
Dmaj7
get some - one to call my lov - er. Yeah, ba - by, come on. Al - right, ba - by, come and
Gmaj7
To Coda
pass my way. I got - ta get some - one to call my lov - er. Yeah, ba - by, come on.
Dmaj7
G
Ay yi, ay yi, ay yi ay yi. Ay yi, ay

Dmaj7
yi, ay yi. Ay yi yi yi. Ay yi, ay yi, ay yi ay yi.
G
1
2
Ay yi, ay yi, ay yi. Ay yi I yi, ay yi. Ay yi yi.
Dmaj7
G
Dmaj7

G
Bm
My my, look - ing for a
F#/A#
Dmaj7/A
Bm/G#
guy guy. I don't want him too shy, but he's got to have the qua - li - ties that
G
D/F#
Em7
D/F#
I like in a man: Strong, smart, af - fec - tion - ate. He's got to be all for me. And I'll
G/A
A
Bm
be too, you see hap - pi - ly.

Gmaj7
D.S. al Coda
CODA
Dmaj7
Al-right, may-be gon-na find him to-day. I got-ta
Gmaj7
Dmaj7
get some - one to call my lov - er. Yeah, ba - by, come on. Al - right, ba - by, come and
Gmaj7
pass my way. I got - ta get some - one to call my lov - er. Yeah, ba - by, come on.

Dmaj7
G
Ay yi, ay yi, ay yi ay yi. Ay yi, ay
Dmaj7
yi, ay yi. Ay yi yi yi. Ay yi, ay yi, ay yi ay yi.
G
Dmaj7
Ay yi, ay yi, ay yi. Ay yi yi. May - be we'll meet at a bar.
Gmaj7
He'll drive a funk - y car. May - be we'll meet at a club and fall so deep - ly in love.

Dmaj7
G
He'll tell me I'm the one and we'll have so much fun. I'll be the girl of his dreams,
Dmaj7
may - be. Al - right, may - be gon - na find him to - day. I got - ta
Gmaj7
Dmaj7
get some - one to call my lov - er. Yeah, ba - by, come on. Al - right, ba - by, come and
Gmaj7
pass my way. I got - ta get some - one to call my lov - er. Yeah, ba - by, come on.

SUPERMAN
(It's Not Easy)

Words and Music by
JOHN ONDRASIK

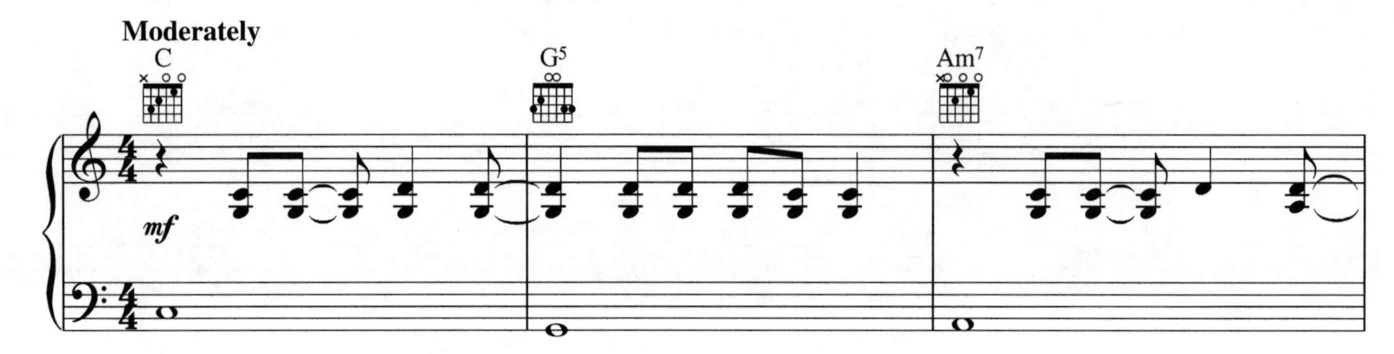

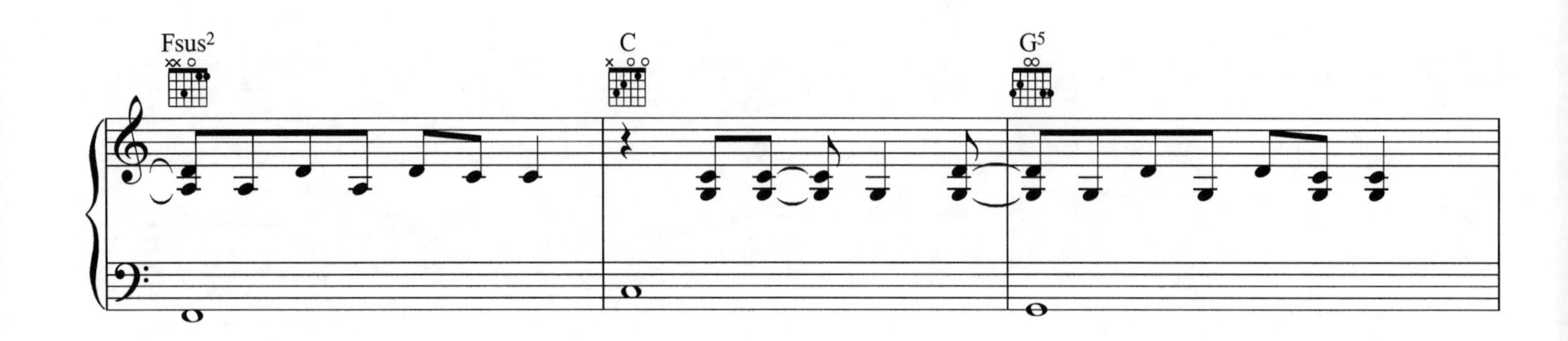

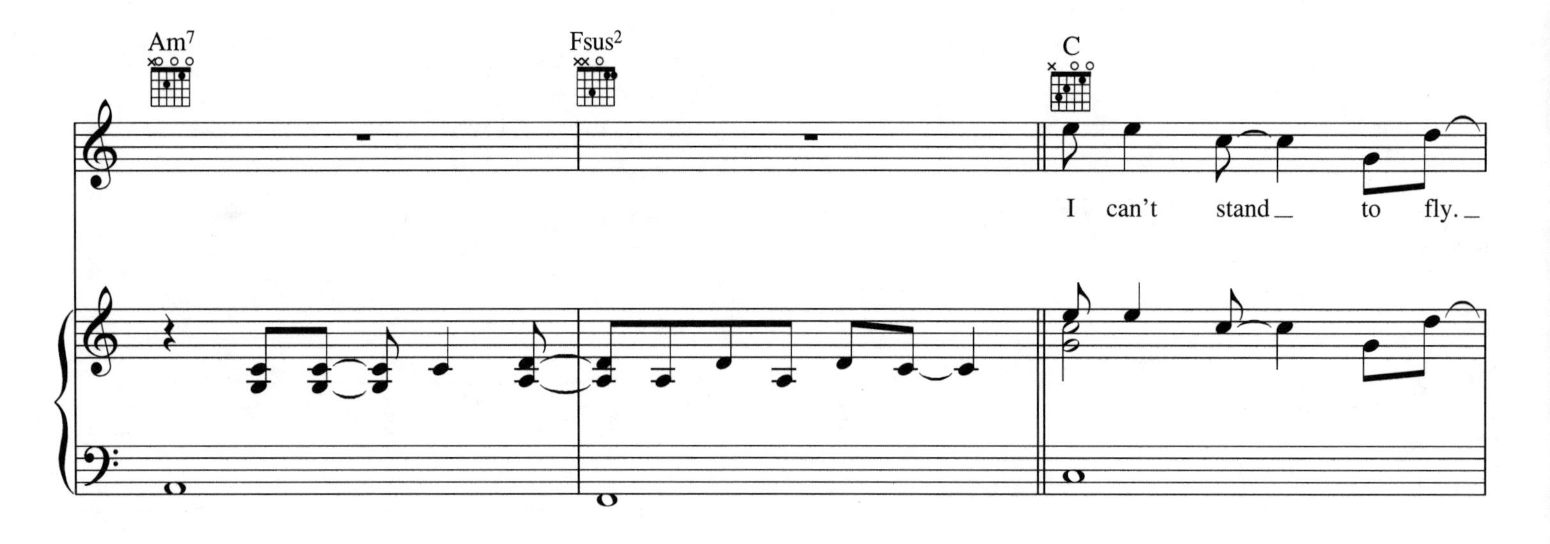

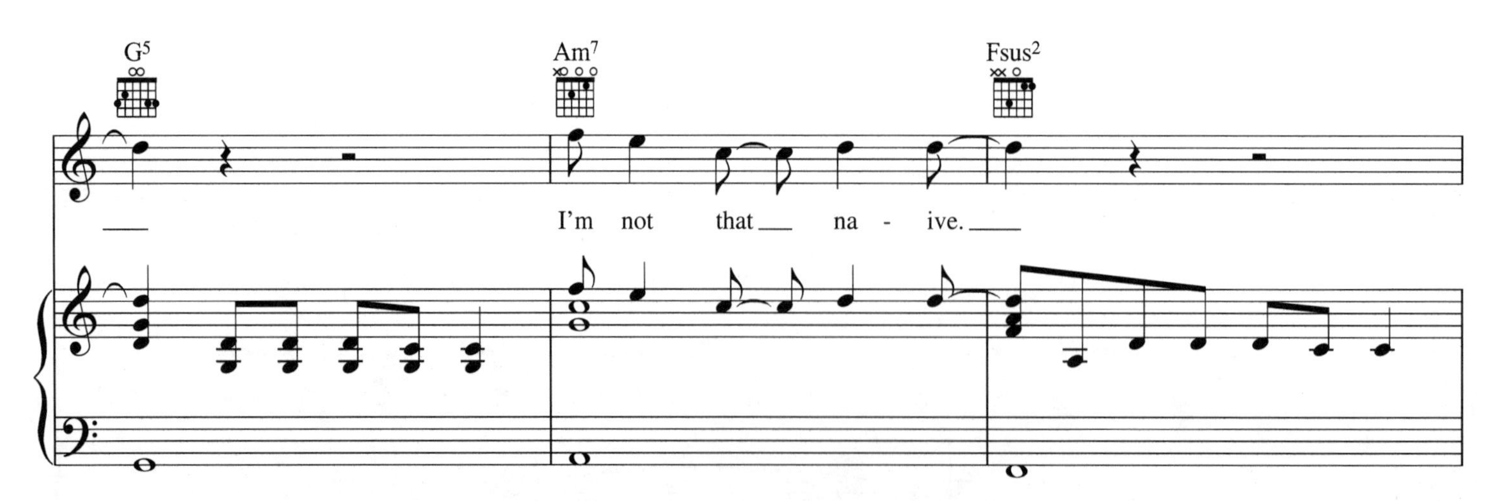

C
G5
Am7
I'm just out to find the better part of me.
Fsus2
C
G5
I'm more than a bird. I'm more than a plane. I'm more than some
Am7
F
C
pretty face beside a train. And it's not easy to be
G
Fsus2
C
me.
I

C
G5
Am7
wish that I could cry.
Fall up - on my knees.
Fsus2
C
G5
Find a way to lie
'bout a home
Am7
Fsus2
C
I'll nev - er see.
It may sound ab - surd,
but don't be na - ive.
G/B
Am7
F
E - ven he - roes have the right to bleed.
I may be dis - turbed,

C
G/B
Am7
but won't you con - cede
e - ven he - roes have the right
F
C
G
to dream? And it's not eas - y to be
Fsus2
C
G/B
Am
G/B
me.
Up, up and a - way,
C
Dm
Am
D
a - way from me.
Well it's all - right,
you can all

C
D
F(add9)
sleep sound to - night. I'm not cra - zy
G
C
or an - y - thing. I can't stand to fly.
G
Am7
Fsus2
I'm not that na - ive.
C
G
Am7
Men weren't meant to ride with clouds be - tween their knees.

Fsus2
C
G5
I'm on - ly a man in a sil - ly red sheet, dig - ging for
Am7
F
C
kryp - ton - ite on this one - way street. On - ly a man in a fun - ny red
G5
Am7
F
sheet, look - ing for spe - cial things in - side of me, in - side of me,
C
G/B
Am7
in - side of me.

F
C
G/B
Yeah, in - side of me, in - side
Am7
F
C
of me. I'm on - ly a man in a fun - ny red
G5
Am7
F
sheet. I'm on - ly a man look - ing for a dream. I'm on - ly a man
C
G5
Am7
in a fun - ny red sheet and it's not eas - y,

Fsus2
Freely
N.C.
C
ooh,
ooh,
ooh.
It's
not
eas -
G
C
- y
to
be
me.
G5
Am7
Fsus2
C

THANK YOU

Words and Music by PAUL HERMAN
and DIDO ARMSTRONG

*Vocal written one octave higher than sung.

Original key: G# minor. This edition has been transposed up one half-step to be more playable.

Am
Fmaj7
G
C
Em/B
and e - ven if I could - it - 'd all be grey, but your pic - ture on my wall,
And e - ven if I'm there - they - 'll all im - ply that I might not last the day,
Am
Fmaj7
Am
Fmaj7
it re - minds me that it's not so bad, it's not so bad.
and then you call me and it's not so bad, it's not so bad. And
1
Am
Fmaj7
Am
Fmaj7
2
C
C/E
Fmaj7
F/G
I want to thank you for giv - ing me the

C
C7
C7/E
Fmaj7
F/G
best day of my life. And
C
C/E
Fmaj7
oh, just to be with you is hav-ing the
Em7
Dm7
best day of my life.
C
C/E
Fmaj7
F/G

C
C/E
Fmaj7
F/G
C
C/E
Fmaj7
F/G
Em7
Dm7
C
C/E
Fmaj7
F/G
Push the door; I'm home at last, and I'm soak - ing through and through.

C
C/E
Fmaj7
F/G
And then you hand - ed me a towel, and all I see is you.
C
C/E
Fmaj7
F/G
And e - ven if my house falls down now, I would-n't have a clue,
Em7
Dm7
be - cause you're near me. And
C
C/E
Fmaj7
F/G
I want to thank you for giv-ing me the

C
C7/E
Fmaj7
F/G
best day of my life. And
C
C/E
Fmaj7
F/G
oh, just to be with you is hav-ing the
Em7
1
Dm7
best day of my life. And
2
Dm7
life.

U GOT IT BAD

Words and Music by USHER RAYMOND,
JERMAINE DUPRI and BRYAN MICHAEL COX

Gmaj7
Bm7
makes you change your ways, _ like hang - in' with your crew, said you act like you're read - y but you don't real - ly know,
Gmaj7
Bm7
and ev - 'ry - thing in your past, __ you wan - na let it go. I've been there, done it, fucked a - round, af - ter
Gmaj7
Bm7
all that, this is what I found. No - bod - y wants to be __ a - lone. If you're
Gmaj7
Bm
touched by the words in this song, then ba - by, you got it, you got it bad when you're on the phone,

Gmaj7
Bm
hang up and you call right back. You got it, you got it bad, if you miss a day
Gmaj7
Bm
A
G
D/F♯
with - out your friend your whole life's off track. Know you got it bad when you're stuck in the house, you don't
Em
A7
Bm
A
G
D/F♯
wan - na have fun, it's all you think a - bout. You got it bad when you're out with some - one, but you
Em
Em/D
C♯m7♭5
F♯7
Bm7
keep on think - in' 'bout some - bod - y else. When you say that you love him and you real - ly know
You got it bad.

Gmaj7
Bm7
ev - 'ry - thing that used to mat - ter, it don't mat - ter no more. Like my mon - ey, all my cars, (you can have it all and)
Gmaj7
Bm7
flow - ers, cards and can - dy, (I do it just 'cause I'm) for - tu - nate to have you, girl. I
Gmaj7
Bm7
want you to know I real - ly a - dore you.
All my peo - ple who know what's go - ing on,
Gmaj7
N.C.
look at your mate, help me sing my song. Fel - las, "I'm your man, you're my girl,

I'm gon - na tell it to the whole wide world." La - dies, "I'm your girl, you're my man.
Bm7
Prom - ise to love you the best I can." See, I've been there, done it, fucked a - round Af - ter
Gmaj7
Bm7
all that, this is what I found. Ev-'ry - one of y'all are just like me. It's too
Gmaj7
Bm
bad that you can't see that you got it... You got it, you got it bad when you're on the phone,

Gmaj7
Bm
hang up and you call right back. You got it, you got it bad, if you miss a day
Gmaj7
Bm
A
G
D/F♯
with - out your friend your whole life's off track. Know you got it bad when you're stuck in the house, you don't
Em
A7
Bm
A
G
D/F♯
wan - na have fun, it's all you think a - bout. You got it bad when you're out with some - one, but you
Em
Em/D
C♯m7
F♯7
Repeat and Fade
Optional Ending
Bm
keep on think - in' 'bout some - bod - y else.
You got it bad.

WHERE THE STARS AND STRIPES AND THE EAGLE FLY

Words and Music by AARON TIPPIN,
CASEY BEATHARD and KENNY BEARD

here's what I tell ev - 'ry - one.
G
Gsus2
I was born by God's dear grace in an
D
ex - tra - or - di - nar - y place.
Where the
Em
G5
3fr
stars and stripes and the ea - gle fly.

D
Dsus2
D
Dsus
D
It's a big ol' land_ with count - less dreams
and hap - pi - ness_ ain't out of reach._
Hard
G
Gsus2
work pays off the way it should._
Yeah, I've seen e -
D
nough to know_ that we've got it good_
where the

Em
D/F♯
G
stars and stripes and the ea - gle fly.
D
Dsus2
D
There's a
C
G
la - dy that stands in a har - bor for what we be -
D
lieve. And there's a

C
G
3
bell that still ech - oes the price that it costs to be
A
D/A
A
N.C.
free.
I
No, it
D
pledge al - le - giance to this flag and if that
ain't the on - ly place on earth, but it's the
both - ers you, well, that's too bad. But if
on - ly place that I pre - fer to

G
you've got pride and you're proud you do,
love my wife and raise my kids,
hey, we could
hey, the
D
use some more like me and you
same way that my dad - dy did:
where the
To Coda
Em
D/F#
G
stars and stripes
and the ea - gle fly.
D

Em
D/F#
G
D
D.S. al Coda
CODA
G
D
and the ea - gle fly.
Em
D/F#
Where the stars and stripes

G
D
N.C.
and the ea - gle
fly.
Dsus
D
Dsus2
D
Dsus
D
Dsus2
D
Dsus
Repeat and Fade
Optional Ending
D
Dsus2
D

WHEREVER YOU WILL GO

Words and Music by ALEX BAND
and AARON KAMIN

Bm7
G6/9
Asus
Dsus2
to light the shad - ows on your face.
through the dark - est of your days.
If a great
Dsus2/C#
Bm7
G6/9
Asus
wave shall fall and fall up - on us all.
D
Dsus2/C#
Bm7
Then be - tween the sand and stone, could you make
Then I hope there's some - one out there who can bring
G6/9
D
it on your own?
me back to you.
If I could,

A
Bm7
G6/9
then I would. I'll go wher - ev - er you will go.
D
A
Bm7
To Coda
Way up high or down low, I'll go wher -
1
G6/9
Dsus2
ev - er you will go. And may - be
2
G6/9
Bm
Gmaj7
ev - er you will go. Run a - way with my heart.

A
F#m
Bm
Run a - way with my hope.
Gmaj7
A
F#m
Run a - way with my love.
D
Dsus2/C#
Bm7
I know now, just quite how my life and love
G6/9
D
Dsus2/C#
might still go on. In your heart, in your mind

Bm
G6
D
D.S. al Coda
I'll stay with you for all of time. If I could,
CODA
G6
D
ev - er you will go. If I could
A
Bm7
turn back time, I'll go wher -
G6
D
ev - er you will go. If I could

A
Bm7
G6/9
make you mine,
I'll go wher - ev - er you will go.
D
A
Bm7
I'll go wher -
G6/9
D
A
ev - er you will go.
Bm7
Gmaj9

YOU ROCK MY WORLD

Words and Music by RODNEY JERKINS,
LASHAWN DANIELS, FRED JERKINS II,
MICHAEL JACKSON and NORA PAYNE

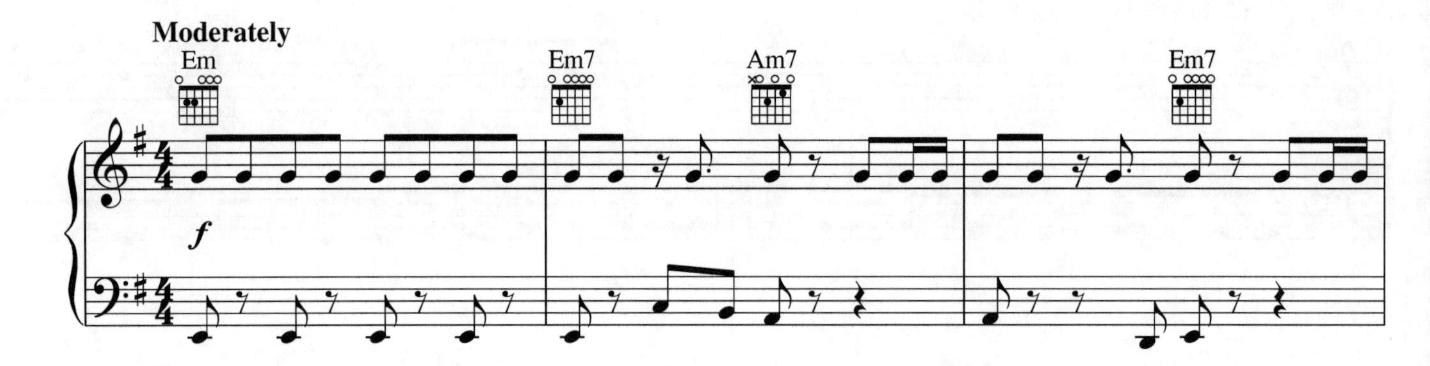

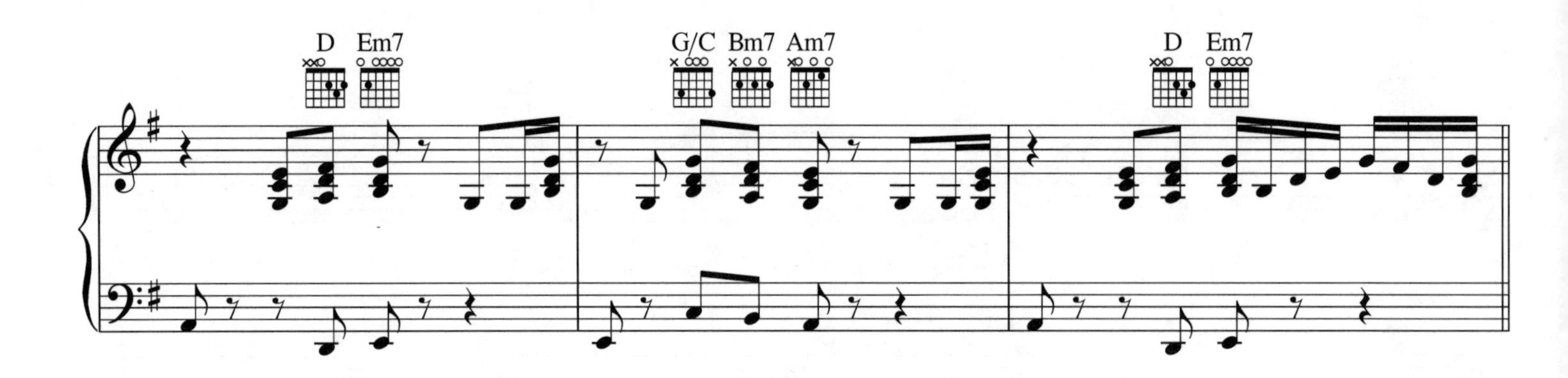

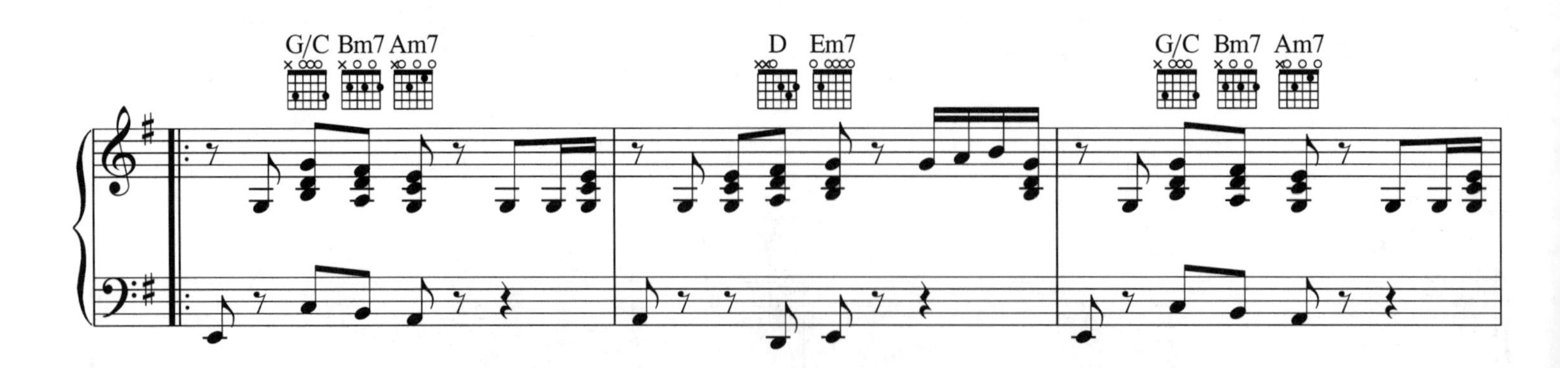

1
D
Em7
2
D
Em7
My
Em
Am
D
Em
life will nev - er be the same 'cause girl, you came and
Am
D
Em
changed the way I walk, the way I talk. I can - not ex -
Am
D
Em
plain these things I feel for you. But girl, you know it's

Am
D
Em
true. Stay with me, ful - fill my dreams and I'll be all you
Oh,
Em7
G/C
Bm7
Am7
D
Em7
ooh, feels so right. I've searched for the
need.
G/C
Bm7
Am7
D
Em7
per - fect love all my life. Oh,
G/C
Bm7
Am7
D
Em7
ooh, feels like I have fin - al - ly

G/C
Bm7
Am7
D
Em7
found a per - fect love this time.
I've fin - al - ly found, so come on,
girl. (You rocked my world, you know you did,
and ev - 'ry - thing I own I give.
The rar - est love, who'd think I'd find
some - one like you to call mine?
You rocked my world, you know you did,
and ev - 'ry - thing I own I give.

G/C
Bm7
Am7
D
Em7
The rar - est love, who'd think I'd find some - one like you to call mine? In
Em
N.C.
Am
D
Em
time I knew that love would bring such hap - pi - ness to
Am
D
Em
me. I tried to keep my san - i - ty; I've wait - ed pa - tient -
Am
D
Em
ly. Girl, you know it seems my life is so com -

Am
D
Em
plete. _ A love that's true be - cause of you. Keep do - in' what _ you
Oh, ___
Em7
G/C
Bm7
Am7
D
Em7
do.
ooh. Think that I've ___ fin - 'lly found the
G/C
Bm7
Am7
D
Em7
per - fect love I've searched for all my life. Oh, ___
G/C
Bm7
Am7
D
Em7
who'd think I'd find ___ such a per - fect

G/C Bm7 Am7
D Em7
love that's awe - some - ly so right.
Oh, girl.
Em7 G/C Bm7 Am7
D Em7
You rocked my world, you know you did,
and ev - 'ry - thing I own I give.
G/C Bm7 Am7
D Em7
The rar - est love, who'd think I'd find
some - one like you to call mine?
G/C Bm7 Am7
D Em7
You rocked my world, you know you did,
and ev - 'ry - thing I own I give.

G/C Bm7 Am7 D Em7
The rar - est love, who'd think I'd find some - one like you to call mine?
G/C Am9 D6 Em9 Bm7
Girl, I know that this is love. I felt
G/C Am11 D Em11 Fmaj9
the mag - ic's all in the air. And girl,
G/C Am9 D6 Em9 Bm7
I'll nev - er get e - nough, that's a - why

C7sus
D7sus
I al - ways have to have you here.
Em7
G/C
Bm7
Am7
D
Em7
You rocked my world, you know you did, and ev - 'ry - thing I own I give,
G/C
Bm7
Am7
D
Em7
The rar - est love, who'd think I'd find some - one like you to call mine?
G/C
Bm7
Am7
D
Em7
You rocked my world, you know you did, and ev - 'ry - thing I own I give.

G/C
Bm7
Am7
D
Em7
The rar - est love, who'd think I'd find some - one like you to call mine?
N.C.
Play 3 times
You rock my
Em
Am
D
Em
world. (You rocked my world, you know you did.) The way you talk to me,
Am
D
Em
the way you're lov - in' me, you, the way you give it to me.

Am
D
Em
(You rocked my world, you know you did.) Give to me.
Yeah, yeah, you, you, yeah, yeah.
You rock my world. You rock my world. You rock my world. You rock my
(You rocked my world, you know you did.)
world. You rock my world. You rock my world. Come on girl.

Em7 G/C Bm7 Am7 D Em7
You rocked my world, you know you did, and ev - 'ry - thing I own I give,
G/C Bm7 Am7 D Em7
The rar - est love, who'd think I'd find some - one like you to call mine?
N.C. G/C Bm7 Am7 D Em7
You rocked my world, you know you did, and ev - 'ry - thing I own I give.
G/C Bm7 Am7 N.C.
The rar - est love, who'd think I'd find some - one like you to call mine?

A WOMAN'S WORTH

Words and Music by ALICIA KEYS
and ERIKA ROSE

Bm7
Em
- by, you know I'm worth it.) Din - ner lit by can - dles, run my bub - ble
- by, I know you're worth it.) If you nev - er play me, prom - ise not to
Bm
Am7
bath, make love ten - der - ly to last and last. (Ba -
bluff, I'll hold you down when shit gets rough. (Ba -
Bm7
Am
G6
D/F♯
Em
- by, you know I'm worth it.) Wan - na please, wan - na keep, wan - na treat your wom - an
- by, I know you're worth it.) She walks the mile makes you smile, all the while be - ing
D
Am
G6
D/F♯
Em
right. Not just dough, but a show that you know she is worth your
true. Don't take for grant - ed the pas - sions that she has for

D Am G6 D/F♯ Em

time. / you. You will lose if you choose to re - fuse to put her

D B7

first. She will, if she can, find a man who knows her

Em7

worth. 'Cause a real man knows a real wom - an when he

Bm7 Am7

sees her, and a real wom-an knows a real man

Bm7
Em7
3
ain't 'fraid to please her. And a real wom - an knows a real man al - ways
Bm7
Am7
comes first, and a real man just can't de - ny
1
Bm7
Em
Bm7
a wom - an's worth. Mm hm mm hm, mm hm mm hm,
Em
Bm7
mm hm mm hm, mm. If you treat me

2
Bm7
Am7
Bm7
Cmaj7
Bm7
Am9
a wom - an's worth.
No need to read be - tween the lines spelled out for you.
Just
3
Am7
Bm7
Cmaj7
Bm7
Am7
hear this song, 'cause you can't go wrong when you val - ue a
B7
(Sing it.)
wom - an's, wom - an's, wom - an's, wom - an's worth.
'Cause a real
Em7
Bm7
man knows a real wom - an when he sees her, and a real
3

Am7
Bm7
woman knows a real man ain't 'fraid to please her. And a real
Em7
Bm7
woman knows a real man always comes first, and a real
Am7
1
Bm7
man just can't deny a woman's worth. 'Cause a real
2
Bm7
Em
a woman's worth. Mm hm mm hm,

Bm7
Em
Bm7
mm hm mm hm,
mm hm mm hm,
mm hm mm hm,
Em
Bm7
Em
mm hm mm hm,
mm hm mm hm,
mm hm mm hm,
Bm7
Em
Bm
mm hm mm hm.
Repeat and Fade
Optional Ending
Am7
Bm7
Bm7
Em